Vit Hopley is a prose writer, artist and editor. Published collections of prose: *Blissful Islands* (2018); *Wednesday Afternoon* (2013); recent video work: *One after the other* (becoming fireflies, 2021).

Yve Lomax is a visual artist, writer and editor. Recent visual work and publications includes *Mad about justice* (becoming fireflies, 2022); *Political Life* (becoming fireflies, 2021); *Nearness* (2019); *Figure, calling* (2018); *Pure Means* (2014).

Here from There is typset in Lora and Myriad Pro

The Copy Press Limited
51 South Street
Ventnor
Isle of Wight
PO38 1NG

copypress.co.uk

loop series

Reader: Belinda Hopley
Copy-editor: Sara Peacock
Design: Opal Morgen / John Peacock
Photographs © Vit Hopley

Front cover © Opal Morgen

Printed on Munken Premium White 90gsm.
Munken Premium White standard products are FSCTM and PEFC certified.

Printed and bound in England by TJ Books Limited, Padstow.

First edition © Copy Press Ltd/ Vit Hopley and Yve Lomax, 2014

Vit Hopley and Yve Lomax assert the moral right to be identified as the authors of this work.

A catalogue record for this book is available from the British Library

ISBN-13 978-1-909570-09-2

All rights reserved. No part of this publication may be reproduced, stored in a retrieval system, or transmitted in any form or by any means, electronic, mechanical, photocopying, recording or otherwise, without the prior permission of the publishers.

This book is sold subject to the condition that it shall not, by way of trade or otherwise, be lent, re-sold, hired out or otherwise circulated without the publisher's prior consent in any form of binding or cover other than that in which it is published and without a similar condition including this condition being imposed on the subsequent purchaser.

HERE FROM THERE

Copy Press *loop*

Vit Hopley · Yve Lomax

A world not yet divided	*13*
A lie not countenanced (Political life)	*15*
Culpable	*19*
A radical equality (That we depend)	*23*
Mystery	*28*
A remarkable opacity (Thinking what we are doing)	*32*
Home	*37*
The unsuccessful pronoun (Not acquiescing to racism)	*39*
Tomorrow today tonight	*43*
A world without appropriation (Justice)	*46*
Pass on	*51*
Dignity knows no bounds (Incalculability)	*54*
Unjudgeable	*59*

Giving with grace (I am because you are, we all are)	*64*
Before	*68*
We need to make another future (Radical love)	*75*
Evermore dense	*80*
Paradise (The walls of incarceration falling)	*81*
Over time	*86*
A rigorous innocence (The cry of the world)	*92*
Memory	*97*
Don't forget language (Remembering the indivisible)	*100*
Gesture	*105*
A life worth living (Free will falls down)	*110*

A world not yet divided

If I am not there, there is a stream at the
bottom of the garden, I am kneeling at the edge
awed by water boatman back swimming; if I'm
not there, I have crossed into the field and I
am under the tree jumping in and out of cow's
hoof prints; if I'm not there, I am in the tree as
high as I can go; if I am not there, I am being
someone else in my world; if I am not there,
the school bus chugs and I am beating its tune
on the back seat; if I am not there, I am drawing
faces in misty windows; if I am not there, I am in
the classroom writing days in joined up letters;
if I am not there, there is a shop that has jars of
coloured sweets, I am wondering which sweet
lasts the longest; if I'm not there,

A lie not countenanced (Political life)

At that time my emotional and intellectual being was directed towards a separation that placed politics on one side and life on the other. I reckoned that politics occupying a space separate from life was questionable. I was no expert, I had no awarded qualifications, but that didn't stop me. It was the separation that bothered me. Politics thus bothered me.

By then I already knew that whatever obtains its basis and legitimacy by constituting itself upon a separation, division or partition wasn't innocent let alone natural. Sexual difference had taught me a lot about that ... when boys and girls come out to play. I knew the first cut was the deepest and nowhere more so than with the activity of management, administration and ordering that gets called government. I had scribbled it down on scraps of paper for later: *government divides itself from the arising of the world to render it governable.*

And then the saddest thing of it all: something getting to be something—*hey, look at me*—by negating others, putting down others, standing on their backs, even the odd neck or two, so as to ground and found themselves and elevate themselves to a projected higher position—*hey, look at me*. This getting to be something on the backs of others was, as still is, tantamount to an origin founded upon negation, exclusion, exploitation. I called it squalid—'squalid origins'. Why not?

What I felt was truly sad (although I suspect the word egregious more fitting) is that the violence of such grounding goes underneath and gets hidden with the *hey look at me* and becomes even more hidden with the normalization of the belief that the backs of those others, from people to planet, are 'material resources' and that it is perfectly okay for them to be used up as their worth is precisely that they can be used up. I had to ask: doesn't that market economy called capitalism, which happily plunders for profit and encourages the standing on the backs of others to get ahead, have squalid origins? Seriously, it needs to stop.

Was I exaggerating when I said that I was putting my heart and soul into querying that separation between politics and life? Not at all. It had felt like a demand to understand that life is only ever found as a *mode*, a way of life. And the word 'only' spoke volumes to me. With it had come the idea—tempted to say *reality*—that nothing of life is separable from its modes. But it didn't

A lie not countenanced (Political life)

stop there. Suddenly I saw that a mode of life, however named, couldn't be encased in a defining outline and taken as distinct. It couldn't.

How come? I gave myself an example. Take a leaf and touch it, even run your fingers around its edge. With this modality of life there is nothing of life to be found in a separate realm. Nothing above, below or before. It is staring you in the face: all of life comes with this mode, this leaf. All of life inhabits this leaf in as much as this leaf inhabits all of life. Life and mode are perfectly coinciding.

The leaf gave me an image of the inseparability of life and its modalities, but I had to add that there is always a situation. It seemed obvious to me that *situations* were going to happen, but it was a lie, a deception and disaster, to think there was a separate realm that politics occupied. I had emphasized the word 'situations' as I wanted to stress that, with nothing of life separable from its modes, political life has always already begun and nothing, not even mother nature, stands apart from it.

There is always a situation and it can be pressing that we have intelligence of it, find the right questions to ask and not back ourselves into a corner. For me, the one thing that political life implicitly calls attention to is squalid origins: that which 'founds' itself or asserts a superiority based on an act of separation, belittlement, negation or sheer violence (… with a sorrow in her voice that's almost unbearable to hear, she sings of blood on the leaves …).

Now a memory is pressing me; it is a memory of words once said, and the memory is coming as a wind, gusts and all, on my back. Remember, remember. I'm going to turn round and have this wind in my face. It is not behind me any more. It is in my face. The wind is in my face. Remember. Remember those words saying that politics names nothing but the *force-relations* of everything that exists. Remember everything is political.

Nothing comes before political life and, for once, this affirms the inseparability of it all.

Culpable

Father, you sit at the head of the table fed
on the trials and tribulations you create:
Godhead?—You are fat! Who decreed that
you sit there fater, vater, fadar, pater,
patēr?—You did!
    Patriarch.
    And his fist hits the table.
    Signalling his authority.
    He sits at the head, son seated on his right,
three daughters there, wife opposite.
    And his fist hits the table.
    Never failing to shock.
    Sharp is the disturbance propagated
through the wooden table and absorbed into
the body.
    And his fist hits the table.

It is always present.
Heralding a division between past and future; fisting before and after.
And his fist hits the table.
Thus, he presides over his family.

And what of the those sitting at his table?
Wife's face no longer gives anything away; son can do nothing else but obey; daughters' body language rigid and tight; and I'm wordless. His family, the embodiment of a lifetime of accusation. And he, clenching knife and fork, cuts and stabs, lifts forkfuls of food to his mouth; his eyes close as he chews; his lips smack with distaste as if something were intolerable.

Something could be anything, language, word, life itself, and it is his, all his. Father—the creator, the protector, the avenger—Patriarch. And something is natural here? Just as actions have consequences and consequences are facts and the fact is he is a big man with high morals who commands respect and anything (and that could be something) that transgresses his command must be wrong, a fault, a crime even. Such authority! and that's a fact. He puts his fork down and pushes away his plate. He breathes heavily.

Something is on his mind.

There it is! His knife stabs air, an interrogation begins, chewing language and words, spittle gathers in the corner of his mouth. The atmosphere is cut with that knife; his family form the background, silent and as inanimate as the crystal decanter on the sideboard. It is his crime scene and everything and everyone present is implicated. Has anyone got anything to say? Speak? Who will dare speak?

One false move, there is always one false move.

And his fist hits the table.

I am the subject of his violence, I am the proof of his attitude, I am the justification of his moralizing judgement. I am wordless. He puts me on trial, he judges and, in his name, condemns me.

Go to Hell!

Father, you create Hell. It is you who condemns life to an ordered line of causal relations; it is your law that justifies itself with accusation. And it is your fist that testifies. Insisting on cause, before and after, that is your hell. Divide and rule, but when all is said and done where is the truth? You might use language to put life in its place, but wrapped around every word there is a silence and no matter how loudly you shout it cannot be said. I am wordless and, in spite of you, I live. The events of life are my chain mail: looped together in links and nodes, what is saved is the right to remain silent, for what cannot be said is the possibility of a future.

Father, life does not begin with you, life does not end with you.

A radical equality (That we depend)

Dependency can be perceived as something not so good. Something has gotten hold of you, got the better of you and you are a slave to it—you name it...social media, techno gadget, computer game, all that intoxicating stuff and that which is purposed to release again and again that little rush of dopamine. Dependency can be contrived and orchestrated. It can be the wife who has no say whatsoever in how her life is lived, is subservient to and at the mercy of an institution, an ideology, a husband. It can be those addictive additives. It can be the fashion that walks down the high street; yes, believe you me, the contrivance is often hidden from you in plain sight. That dependency can be contrived means something is going on that is far from innocent.

Dependency as something not so good takes us toward passivity if not touches passion in the old-fashioned sense of suffering. But let's take dependency and turn it in the direction of a different perception. Not in the direction of self-sufficiency and independence, which is, let's face it, mythical yet nonetheless the apogee of 'man' and his 'masculinity'; rather, dependency as the very condition of our existence, the fabric of our being, and by that I don't only mean human beings. I mean *everything* …

There was a televised interview with the political scientist Bruno Latour and the words and thoughts being transmitted were not falling on deaf ears. I was listening, although truth be told, I was reading subtitles, pausing, rewinding and scribbling things down. Okay, some of the sentences became a little scrambled but he did say something like this: we depend—it is a good thing. In fact, we are what we depend upon, and it makes us interdependent.

I depend—it is a good thing. We all depend, everything depends, and that's to say interdependency is the condition of our existence. And I get it that knowing this, understanding and embracing this, is emancipatory.

Interdependency situates you, which is indeed to say you are that upon which you depend, but stuff depends on you, your actions and, yes, your non-actions. Your existence inextricably involves others; it has an impact on others. Bruno Latour wanted to demonstrate this; he talked about following the network of your dependency—to think about it, to write it down. In the process, contrary to being overwhelmed, you'll see that you are a capacity to act, and I'll add that, in the process, you'll also see an

A radical equality (That we depend)

unmaking of borders and boundaries. In many respects this is precisely it: interdependency shows you over and over again that there is no border between you and the world and all that comes to constitute and compose it. Following the network of your dependency what comes is an intimacy with what has seemed so distant, so far away and nothing whatsoever to do with you.

The air that I breathe depends and I depend on it—air belongs to no one and everyone. Interdependency profoundly and often beautifully undoes—better still, does not make—borders and boundaries. I had avoided using the word interdependency. I couldn't rid myself of an image of two or more separate things linked by a relation of dependency. Then I saw *inclinations* and the image held my attention. In our very being we are inclined and this intwines us, and that is *everything* ...

Following on from her infamous troubling of gender, Judith Butler has been saying that we have got to start avowing interdependency. We've got to dismantle rigid forms of individuality, for the sake of a new idea of equality and an understanding that what a body is occurs in its dependency on other bodies and a shared world. It is 2022 and in *The Force of Non-Violence* she says it more than once... 'a new idea of equality can only emerge from a fully imagined interdependence... Equality is thus a feature of social relations that depend for its articulation on an increasingly *avowed* interdependency...I have been arguing that the task, as I imagine it, is...to accept interdependency as a condition of equality.'

It is staring us in the face, but some still go to great pains to deny and disregard interdependency. They disavow that they depend. They disavow that our lives and bodies are bound up with lives and bodies of others, and not just human. It is interdependency that makes existence possible and interdependency thwarts us picturing a world filled with separate things. My existence is caught up with so much and, whichever way I picture it, borders and boundaries keep slipping away, and it is okay; it is a good thing—it brings *being* equal, and it never stops coming. And the fundamental thing that happens here is that *equality* isn't attached or fastened to individually separate and distinct bodies; rather, equality spreads to everything. Better still: with borders and boundaries slipping away equality spreads *through* everything.

I had already written it down some time ago:

'I cannot think of equality as a possession, something belonging to bodies as units, measurable and calculable. Equality is extremely radical; it spreads through everything and is profoundly incalculable. But saying this I am not at all denying the brutal mutilation, cruelty and violence done to bodies, be they of flesh and blood or wood and water.'

A radical equality (That we depend)

Equality can't be converted into a property or possession. It can't be taken as one's own. It simply can't. Equality can only be as a 'state of the world'. And that is acknowledging and holding dear a shared world, that everything depends on everything and that it is a good thing.

Mystery

Why the architect became a monk is a mystery. And how it was that the monk happened to be an architect is a mystery. Did the architect, before deciding to become a monk, have a plan? And the monk, did he have a plan? Monk architect: monk and architect falling together, divinely human.

The monk architect built Quarr Abbey.

And he decided to build in brick. Brick, the common brick, man-made to fit in the hand; and he chose not just any brick but a particular brick—small, rough Flemish brick for its warm reds and yellows, earthly as from the beginning; and in each brick made, fired handprints become trace fossils. And he used plenty. Two million bricks. Brick by brick by brick laid by hand, set apart together and the Abbey, with its interior buttresses, high arches supporting the roof, and two towers, was built in brick alone.

The Abbey.

Outside, the fact of each brick testifies to its building; inside, light through small yellow glass windows glows, the mix of colour and hue taking the Abbey to the arché. And monks robed in black move about reflected through shadow and reposed through silence. A monk's life, a rule of life, lived in prayer, in contemplation, prostrate and not from here. It is a mystery.

And life is it ever by design? I am at a crossroads, forever at a crossroads, and I am not the only one: going over and over before and after before then; facts speaking louder than words, it is an eternal drama. Life. How I judge! I take a pew and I am not the only one looking from the outside looking in. There I am looking to the past for understanding as though it were the cause of all things. Am I not the author of my life? Did I not decide then and then and then—it's history!—And then? Inside

looking in, there I am at a threshold, in crisis.
What next? Putting then aside even though it
is now, what is manifest has never been; before
and after falling together and rising up without
design is a mystery.

    The Abbey was it built for this? The Abbey,
each brick chosen, handed over, is its gesture
over and over again; and all that action coming
together hollows into bare warmth. Inside.
The nave is immense. I am there, a fact of
then, going over and over before and after.
A monk passes through the Abbey. Moving
silently. And there, a confrontation of shadow
and silence—shadows or afterimages or black
habits? In the air burnt incense is redolent,
an atmosphere not from here lingers. Outside
in. I am there, immersed in a warm glow, and
bird song begins to fill the nave; and then an
apparition—a black cat pouncing and leaping
with its tail curling; a black cat chasing shadows
all the way to the high altar to forever dissolve
in golden light.

    This is the truth. I testify to myself. Going

Mystery

over and over, before and after before then,
what takes me here (a moment of elaboration:
bricks, reds, yellows, glow, aroma, monk,
bird, shadow, cat: a moment arising) is not
of here. This is the truth. Over and over,
before and after before then, there is here
and there is elsewhere; there is someone
and there is someone else: there, a decisive
confrontation—the temporal and the eternal
falling together—and it's divinely human. This is
the truth. I am not myself today. What a drama!
And there, the authority to write this word by
word by word.

A remarkable opacity
(Thinking what we are doing)

In a world that valorizes transparency, opacity is to be eschewed, disavowed, purged. No surprises here. In fact, the valorization of transparency creates its own world. It is the easily seen through. It is the open plan. The imaginary of this world is to show the whole thing as and when it happens, how it comes about and with what. Everything is taking place in the open and everyone can see it. And what is repugnant to this imaginary is the conniving behind closed doors, shady deals, secret alliances, purposeful obscurations.

Transparency and openness have become so close as to be synonymous and I cannot forget the insidious situation that together they can create. And it happens when the valorization of transparency creates its world yet, for all the good riddance to corruption and secrecy, flips into a regime. And this happens when, every minute of the day, transparency requires everything to be accountable, assessable, auditable, measurable. What creeps in here and creeps all over is something best named control. It is creepy, and not because something lurks in the shadows but, rather, because everything is taking place in the open, in plain sight. It is pernicious.

There are the thick black lines that strike through the written record of a meeting gathered for the sake of governance, government or business; the darken (*opacus*) page of the redacted text and it shows it clearly: here is an opacity that shows something not to be seen. Yet there is another opacity that shows no such thing. I'm calling it a *remarkable opacity*.

More must be said of this opacity; I know that. And to do this let me say: life cannot be conceived except as existing. Life has to be generated so as to exist and to exist life has to be generated. Yet we can't assume that anything of life is there *before* existing. It is not the case that before existing life 'brought to pass that it was to be'—that's not the nature of life.

It may seem obvious that forms and modes of life are generated through and by life; perhaps less obvious is that the generative 'life' isn't to be found before or external to the generated. This is the crux of the matter: the generative doesn't come *before* and the generated doesn't come *after*. No one, not even the bright shiny ones, can finally settle or determine which comes first and which follows after.

So, it's not a straightforward temporality where *after*

(present or future) follows *before* (past). Rather, what comes is something like a generative temporality, more a matter of *what life will have been in the process of what life is becoming*.

Simply put, the generative and the generated can't be separated from each other and the situation brings an indeterminacy and, what's more, there is no going beyond it. I haven't hit a brick wall or anything like that, and there is neither tears nor anger. Rather, I have come to the opacity that I'm calling remarkable. And remarkable for the very reason that with this opacity there is no obscuration, no concealment, no hoodwinking, no sleight of hand, no failure of erudition or intelligence, none whatsoever.

Just by existing, you are both life generated and generative of life and it means that an opacity, not the dark opposite of transparency, is internal to your existence. There is your sorrow, there is your joy and then there is your opacity, which is equally shared by all that is life. What I do have to say (and perhaps keep on saying) is that this opacity, for all the no-going-beyond it, doesn't make me poor in insight. Quite the opposite. As soon as I clocked it, a clarity came and it felt good that this opacity was not a barrier to thinking. And pretty quickly I realized that, with it, what was scuppered was something assuming a first place, an 'originary' place—and that is to say, an 'origin' with which a 'command' comes that continuously orders what develops, making it always answerable to it. And seeing this *not* happening, what I have been given insight into is the shenanigans that do go on for such a 'first place' to be assumed. And add to this, 'superior one'. Indeed, the indistinction of what comes first and what follows after has thrown into relief the conniving of that which establishes itself by the putting down and negation of another—and so often does not hesitate to impose itself through violence.

Here comes the big-I-am, the better-than-you, the all-important-one sitting at the head of the table; here comes the invader, the colonialist, the misogynist; here comes the birth of a nation; here comes supremacy and segregation; here comes apartheid, genocide, femicide; here comes the criminality of the state, the treatment of migrants, revulsion towards and abuse of.

I say it simply, not lightly and out loud almost howling: didn't anyone think what they were doing? Stupid to think I am going to get a response.

Didn't anyone think what they were doing? I cannot deny how extensive the violence is, but I cannot deny how extensive that remarkable opacity is: the indistinction between what in life generates and what is generated is everywhere. And everywhere it is happening across things. *This* is generated by *that* and *that* is generated by *this*; what is generative of another is generated by another—things are happening across (trans) and we truly can't say what comes before and what comes after. What also transpires is an undoing of divisions and separations between entities and 'identities'. Then I get it: that remarkable opacity is soliciting us to think the involvement that is happening here; yes, it is soliciting us to think and to think what we are doing.

And if this is not ethics then I don't know what is.

Jacqueline Rose, in *On Violence and On Violence Against Women*, 2021, puts it simply: 'There are guns, and there is thinking.'

Home

Home: a high stone wall patched with hedge and bits of fence; its gate, wrought iron, unlocks to wide steps leading to the home; its grounds protected, enclosed; inside—narrative freely folds time and space—the garden, the playground, the tree, the grassy mound and children; the children, put here for safe keeping; rosy cheeks slapped on the face; inside, frozen stars. They are playing, so it seems, 'it'.
　— Who's it?
　It, stinking black hole from the gut, tongue smacking 'it' against clenched teeth: it's screaming.
　— She's it.
　She: stood on the grassy mound in the sun; her head tipped back, eyes closed, hands cupping ears: spots and flashes radiate in darkness, turbulences enmesh together, her

breath draws internal pictures of volcanoes, earthquakes.

— She's it.

She: fell on her knees in the playground; she sits with grazed knees brought up under her chin: her knees, celestial landscapes covered in craters mixing blood and grit; dry-eyed, she flicks grit into outer space.

— She's it.

She: ran to the shelter of the beech tree; under its dark canopy she cuts skin deep a delicate bark unable to heal itself: there is no escaping it, thick-skinned is the name that remains to be seen.

— She's it.

The unsuccessful pronoun
(Not acquiescing to racism)

The story goes that pronouns come along to save you from having to say a name or noun repeatedly. What pronouns do is to stand 'in place of'; yet for pronouns to perform accordingly and successfully we have got to know what is and has been going on. We have to know what has already been said, and sometimes it is a matter of knowing what is just about to be said.

If I were to say 'This is going to break your heart' what would you make of this, *this* that is going to break your heart? Perhaps 'this' names something that doesn't know how to have its name spoken—and it pains. Maybe it is a case of what is struggling to be born as having only *this* as shelter for its fragile existence. With the (demonstrative) pronoun 'this' we look to find what is near and to what it is referring yet, for all of our poetic imagination, the *this* that is going to break your heart is unsuccessfully referring.

For sure, there is a craft in the placing of a pronoun and the referring that comes with it. Tricky you must admit. But there is something else: pronouns are loaded.

Do I need to speak of those gendered personal pronouns? These pronouns—not only are they charged but they are also a weight some desperately prefer not to bear. Found in brackets after a proper name (he/his), they signify deliberate personal decisions—make no mistake about it. Loaded, yes. And then there is the use of 'they' expressing the desire for pronoun gender neutrality, which in itself is not a new phenomenon.

They most certainly want to shed the load and to be neither or both her or him and, moreover, said in the singular. But what about 'we'? How can 'we' shed its load, for it most certainly has one? Over the years I have become attuned to hearing the assertion of dominance in the utterance of 'we'. I've heard a 'we' seeking determinacy through the action of exclusion, which this 'we' justifies so as to make it 'proper', although all the ingredients are present for this 'we' to have a sordid foundation. I've heard the 'we' of a dominant order who is, in saying 'we', going to speak for everyone, no matter what. And then I have heard a 'we' doing everything it can to assert itself and be recognized rather than excluded, negated or spoken for, and the justification for this recognition comes on the basis of reparation for oppression, degradation, disrespect, discrimination—who hasn't felt this?

Here is the question—how can 'we' be said without there being any exclusion or negation? The political

The unsuccessful pronoun (Not acquiescing to racism)　　　　*41*

theorist Achilles Mbembe says it like this: for the name 'Earth', the pronoun is 'we'. In the conclusion to *The Earthly Community*, 2022, he asserts:

'… the last utopia involves coming back to the Earth, the last name of a *we* that would embrace human beings as well as objects, viruses, plants, animals, oceans, machines—all the forces and energies with which we must now learn to live in *bio-symbiosis*. The greatest obstacle to the idea of a "we" is, however, racism, the ultimate neurosis of separation. As a singular form of war of the species, racism is indeed the exact opposite of any consciousness of the common. It must be added that in order to be truly universal, the fight against various forms of racism must not be put at the service of the power politics of states. It must be put at the service of truth, justice, and reconciliation between all the species of the living. It is … in these terms of mutuality, of solidarity, of recognition of our common vulnerability that I imagine the new *we*, or what has been called the *in-common*.'

We isn't human (*anthro*) centric; we that are the Earth is not constituted by an act of exclusion or expulsion but racism is. Racism—so pernicious, ugly and brutal—relishes the cut that puts in place, on either side, the pronouns 'us' and 'them'. Racism strains to keep those pronouns in place and knowing exactly to what they are referring. Racism gives *them* no love, at best false smiles.

For *we*, 'us' and 'them' are *in-common*. Us and them slip into one another and this lets me write: them are all those forms of life, ways of being, forces and energies that are us. Them is the Earth that is us. And with that said, pronouns come to enjoy success of a completely different order.

Tomorrow today and tonight

I row out onto the lake and the world opens up. Everything is as it should be: sky above and lake below, night and day; each day returning onto the lake, sunlight sent back, beneath its surface a current of darkness. The wind held in trees around its shore is almost still. Yesterday is a long way off, as is tomorrow.

The wooden rowboat kept tied to the end of the jetty bobs about as I get in, almost rocking me off balance. I have been given a fishing rod and tackle: I have everything I need to go fishing and I have thought no further than this—*I have never been fishing before.*

I row out until the jetty recedes, disappearing into the shoreline; detached, there I am sitting in the small wooden rowboat on the lake tying a lure to a fishing line. The lure, a spinnerbait, has a silvery disc with a red wiggle and orange diamond painted on it; the hook has three prongs.

I cast out, again and again making circular ripples on the still lake. I reel in again and again and get nothing back. An empty plastic container, an old ice cream tub, rolls about on the bottom of the boat. Should there be a hole in the boat I can always bail out. Yes! I could swim back too.

Everything is as it should be in a rowboat: sky above, lake below, silent and still, all enclosed in fresh air. I sit on the bench in the middle of the boat untangling the fishing line. The old ice cream tub, now filled with water, has been placed beside me on the bench. If I catch a fish I want to put it in water.

I try again. Casting out reeling in, again and again; the fishing line a straight line slices through darkness; out there nothing is willing to be lured into the light of day. Eventually, of course when least expected, the lure, a silvery disc with a red wiggle and orange diamond painted on it, is bitten and the line becomes taut.

Reeling the line in, I feel resistance; there brought up to the surface, lashing out of clear darkness are stripes, colour, intense green and yellow; and so quickly an energy, all agitation, breaks loose. And so quickly, freely dispersing, what is frenetic dissolves; the line becomes slack and the moment absorbs the stillness of the lake.

I stand up, the boat rolls gently; water spills over the brim of the ice cream tub. The fishing rod lies discarded on the bottom of the boat, and my feet are wet; there is a large bird chasing its shadow across the lake.

A world without appropriation (Justice)

I'm not sure how many people would agree that so much of the world is treated as an object of utility. Even though I hope most do, I can't say. But what I can say is that before utility is extracted from an 'object' somewhere along the line an act of appropriation, perhaps several, will have taken place. To appropriate is to take as one's own and do what you please. And there is one thing that an act of appropriation speaks of and it is separation—what is appropriated is taken as, treated as, separate. And separation *thus* is precisely what occurs and recurs with what has been called an 'object'.

Objects of utility—you don't need to be a visionary to see the appropriation that turns the beauty of each and all, of planet and people, into objects to extract the maximum utility (and profit) from. So much of the Earth and its inhabitants have been *captured* to become an object of utility: rain forests hacked down, land ravaged by mining and left exhausted, intensive farming (animals included), seabeds trawled and ruined, the very bowels of the Earth disgorged and, in so many ways and for so long, women. Yes, so much capture that belittles and sacrifices lives for the betterment and enjoyment of others. Yes, so much appropriation leading to extraction, exploitation and depletion.

And to the list (it is longer than I can imagine) I must add the capture of education and learning as it is subjected to the quantification of knowledge and the endless assessment of 'impact' (utility). It wears down and depletes the curiosity and desire of the soul. And then there are those thousand and one electronic gadgets and items, along with ever increasing computing technologies, calling out to be utilized yet, in so doing, turn the tables such that what is captured—and I'll even say appropriated—is now the user. The user is possessed and look no further than the ubiquitous mobile phone—we know it and we abandon ourselves to it.

This is not the first time that I have thought of appropriation and I know it won't be the last. Some time ago, my attention (if not love) was called by the question: isn't it time to embrace the world *in so far as it is inappropriable?* And now the question returns and an urgency comes with it. No wonder given the damage done by the unremitting attack of appropriation on the world. And by 'world' I mean the Earth, its habitats and inhabitants. There are perhaps many 'worlds' but there is only one Earth (as far as we know) and it is priceless. To treat the Earth as inappropriable is not impossible. Before utility and profit became the decisive word on all things, it happened. It can happen and in places it is happening.

I'm going to say that, by definition, the Earth is inappropriable. No one can own it, even if a powerful and persuasive imaginary believes that ownership and private property is a natural right. For this imaginary the Earth is reduced to appropriated land around which boundaries are erected. And then comes war. In these appropriated lands, humanity (if indeed that word can be said) is at war not only with itself but also with habitats and environments. That's to say, humanity is at war with nature. It is worth crying about. Yet what the Earth truly is I shall never know and for the very reason that the Earth is potential; in other words, the Earth is a capacity. Earth is a *capacity* for habitat and inhabitation. And this capacity is incalculable.

To treat the Earth as inappropriable opens the way to repair the damage done by the extraction of maximum utility; it brings about a reversal of the action of 'taking possession and making one's own' and, with that, an understanding of a 'making use' that is counter to utility, extraction and ownership.

—Can *we*?

A world without appropriation (Justice)

It was by accident that the book fell open at that page, unless of course magic or a guardian angel was at work, which if they were (and I don't dismiss either one) I am grateful, for what was brought to my attention was truly unexpected and, I must add, just at the right time.

The book had been well used, open and shut many times and with certain passages read repeatedly. The book: *The Use of Bodies*, 2015, written by the philosopher Giorgio Agamben. At the top the page, I hear about a brief text by the critical theorist and philosopher Walter Benjamin called 'Notes toward a Work on the Category of Justice', 1916. The title of the chapter is 'The Inappropriable', the page number is 81 and I'm all ears.

And there at the top of the page I read that Benjamin makes a close connection between justice and inappropriability; it is to do with possession (in fact, possessionless) and the good. Simply put, possession is always unjust: 'No order of possession, however articulated, can ... lead to justice. Rather, this lies in the condition of the good that cannot be a possession. This alone is the good through which goods become possessionless.' Justice and the good coincide.

For no one can the good be a possession. No one can own it. That the good comes to be, that it can be, is justice. Justice is ethical and it pertains to *existence*. That's to say, justice is (akin to equality) a 'state of the world'. It is, in the words of Benjamin, 'the striving to make the world into the highest good'. The condition of the good involves no appropriation and to make the world—the Earth and *we* that are it—supremely good means to experience it, to treat it, as inappropriable. That is justice for you—and it is urgent.

Pass on

This eventuality had been waiting for me.
    Mother, first born.
    Must I be here? Today. In this room. Small and dark. A succulent occupies the deep windowsill; light barely reaches in. There are three chairs, in three corners; a small lacquered table; and a picture—a galleon on turbulent seas making history, sails and flags puffed out with wind. Those of noble thought, guided by the antiquated map of town and harbour on the opposite wall, would say 'what year is this? Was it then or was it then? Who was capturing who? Pirates, traders, captains and admirals! Heroic times, victorious times propel us forward, how could we forget?' Forget?

Port Mahon. The walls are thick, the port is fortified; the walls are thick, the room is soundproof. Shell ears. Outside, the sun beats down, hotting up; inside, finding a way in, footsteps resonate down marble corridors—coming towards, going away; coming towards, going away. The walls are thick. Outside, someone picks over some ruins thinking they have got somewhere today; inside, I trace the outline of my head silhouetted against the small lacquered table; intimate and familiar, I see mother's shadow.

My hands are mother's and the shape of my head—mother, here I am! an empty featureless shape standing in your bright light. Mother prepared for this day: before and beyond she saw today coming. Before now, mother waited here, in this room, with her life in her hands, holding all that she had about her and all that she would pass on. Did she admire the map; did she put her bag down on that chair; did she tut the plant pot's dryness and then squeeze its spongy leaves; did she lean on this table? Did she? Mother came here to lodge her will and now she is dead her will brings me.

Mother. And the room gets smaller. Looking into the silhouette memories arise, passed from generation to generation, up and down the family tree; a potted history, how can I forget? Looking back a ghosting, mother, mother's mother, mother's mother's mother; that head, those hands; tracing ancestry, how far back can I go? Mother coming towards, going away; coming towards, going away; she has brought me here and I have followed—teardrops pool.

Tears glisten in darkness, a sparkling light for every moment lost and forgotten. Mother, there you are! wiping away my tears, making way for the future ahead of me. The atmosphere is close. On the windowsill, leaves broken free from the succulent are rooting in nothing. Mother! guard me from myself for today will have been.

Dignity knows no bounds (Incalculability)

The quantification of the Earth, all that composes it and peoples it, has become so extensive; I'm tempted to say, immense. Do I have the means to calculate this? I don't, but calculation is the very issue and I perceive it each time I find myself in a 'computational' situation. Each time I switch on, log on, click on, scroll and go looking, I *feel* calculation on a scale that leaves me almost breathless.

The Earth, life and living, are taken to be calculable and quantifiable; in fact, by way of ever faster computer technology, they are—*we* are—preyed upon to yield data and thus treated as 'computable objects'. And it is not wrong to see this treatment, and the 'harvesting' or 'mining' of data that comes with it, as *extraction*. So much data is extracted—from land, sea, forests, bodies to every action performed with the computer technology woven into the habits and things of daily life. And as the data is bought and sold, further extractions are set to happen, including predictive calculations for a futures market. Yes, so much 'captured' by data extraction and if you don't yield data you are, whatever you are, deemed worthless. I don't think I am exaggerating.

Life, lives and living, are 'weighed' by calculations that sort out the worthless from the profitable; it is worth repeating: if no calculation can be fixed and no quantification is forthcoming, you are, whatever—and *however*—you are, deemed worthless. Reasoning backwards and one thing leading to another, it means that the worthless have an incalculable value and that, so I'm hearing, defines *dignity*.

Towards the end of *What World Is This?*, 2022, Judith Butler says that we can assert the incalculable value of life without a firm definition of life; she goes on to quote Jacques Derrida from 'The "World" of the Enlightenment to Come', 2003, who is citing Emmanuel Kant from *The Metaphysics of Moral*, 1797. In this quote, Derrida says that rationality 'has never been limited, as some have tried to make us believe, to calculability'. He also says that the role 'dignity' plays in Kant 'belongs to the order of the incalculable' and is opposed to what has a price on the market. Incalculability grabs my attention and, with that, dignity. Dignity has an incalculable value and introducing a twist to make it not exclusively human nor anything to do with autonomy I can say that the dignity of the Earth, of life and living, is precisely its worthlessness, its pricelessness, its incalculability.

What of the dignity of justice? There is no denying the question implies that justice is incalculable, but how can this be the justice that is the exercise of law and right—*droit*. It isn't. Rather, it is the justice calling out in an intense text by Jacques Derrida, which came together between the late 1980s and the early 1990s, called 'Force of Law: "The Mystical Foundation of Authority"'. This justice is irreducible to law, but, at the same time, doesn't give itself over to the making of a stable, unequivocal, hard and fast distinction between itself and law. That said, we have to remind ourselves that law is always an authorised force.

There would be no law without rules. Rules must apply and with their applicability law accounts for itself; in one way or another, it is a matter of calculation. Law is the element of calculation. And then there is the enforcement of law; for sure, there are laws that aren't enforced and of course law varies from land to land, but it is clear: there is no law without enforceability. What's more—and this truly is no surprise—there is no enforcement without force, be it direct, indirect, physical, symbolic, coercive, subtle or brutal.

Here is the thing, justice isn't insured by a rule. Law must have the power to 'apply a rule, enact a program or effect a calculation' but that is not justice. There is the justice of law, justice as law and then there is justice.

Dignity knows no bounds (Incalculability)

We can't calculate justice—I hear that, but I'm thinking that justice needs time. Even though the act has been done and the damage inflicted, justice needs, I'll even say demands, that time given over to it 'will have been'. Although done, not yet is the damage inflicted in the past. It 'will have been', but not yet. It is something like a future being 'shadowed by a past struggling to be born'. The future perfect (some say future anterior) gives us, gives justice, time to think, to see and even 'deconstruct' what is involved. It can be the hardest thing to do. What I do know is that no calculation or quantification can be brought to bear upon this time; in advance, no one can say it will take a couple of hours, a few days or many months. The future perfect gives justice the time it needs and it's like being touched lightly and given something in your hand that you know in your heart so much depends upon, and it does come as a gift. A gift without exchange.

What is needed in this time is an eye that sees in the fullest sense. It is not calculation, but it is recognition, vision. Seeing what is not yet 'will have been' is to see the corpses still lying blood stained in the streets, the persisting pain caused by lucrative crops replacing the irreplaceable lives of trees and the forest they make and the life it supports AND it is having the vision to see how reparation, healing and making good can come to be.

Without recognition of the pain and damage inflicted, there can be no reparation, no 'will have been'. And there is something that is tough: reparation for the irreparable.

No one is saying that the time given to justice and for justice doesn't bring urgency and decisions. For all the equivocations (there are no 'right' rules to follow), decisions are to be made. You go through the ordeal of not knowing if the decision will be just or unjust, yet you are deciding. And in the instant of deciding, there is always an urgency. NOW! Without this ordeal and this urgency there would only be the 'programmable application or unfolding of a calculable process'. I can't deny the madness in it. Jacques Derrida said he was mad about justice. He also said that, in justice, we can recognize a madness.

That you can't calculate your way out of it and having no programme or rules to apply, but still needing to decide, is madness, yet this madness bears the dignity of justice in as much it bears the dignity of the Earth. It holds out for all that is unquantifiable and incalculable and, what's more, holds out for the Earth to be *not* treated or appropriated as a vast marketplace. And with the madness that bears the dignity of the Earth a call rumbles; it is for a new law on Earth.

Unjudgeable

I learned yesterday.

It went by many names—slow worm, legless lizard, deaf adder, blind worm, long-cripple.

It was a black line moving in long grass. I saw it. It was a coil around itself, writhing. I found it. It was burrowing between warm stones. It blinked at me.

The next morning, I chased lines in the grass. I was carrying a small basket with a lid, which I had found in a box amongst other things that might have a use. The basket was hand woven from straw. The sun was bright. What was my hope? It would appear. And it would voluntarily curl up into the basket? How charming! It was nowhere. After a time, I returned to the spot where the stones were warm. I nestled the empty basket between them.

Here was once a garden and is at once a garden; this garden, a lost place, collapsing in on itself, was given over to nature: before a ground cleared and walled for cultivation and after left to its own design. An earthly paradise. And there, under a big sky, I sat amongst grasses, lively, on a slope banking down to a lake edged with rushes. And behind, a house bound with woody vines laced with thorns sat within its wilderness of grasses, flowers, apple trees and crumbling stone walls. And behind that, a forest of pines, deep and dark and tall, pierced the sky.

And the sun shone down on me. How could I not resist the temptation to stretch out and laze in its warmth. My eyelids fluttering against its brightness, folded the outside in. Inside my hollowed skull black space irradiated, sound and sensation amplified shaping a place not yet from here, not yet from now—breathing, rustling, buzzing, flapping, rumbling—a vertiginous place without word, an auditorium before its event. I could neither open nor close my eyes and from there I fell into a deep sleep.

Unjudgeable

I dreamt in a darkness that I did not know was possible, a darkness thick with matter. And this darkness was such that I could not see myself; nightmare or dream, I knew I was not dead; life was coursing through me, thoughts flashed black folds in my brain; but where was I? In a black desert, being freed from being in the world was a self without outline, autonomous without representation. Anarchic. And here was darkness at the beginning and end of time, the time that surrounds everything that is possible. Heaven or Hell, here was nowhere, without bound but not without gravity.

Onward I wandered, each step stepping deeper and deeper in darkness. I could not see my way, there was not a path to follow, yet I did not feel lost; something was calling me, calling me to go further and further. And the further I went the darkness became thicker, more leaden, more substantial; I felt its burden and knew I could go no further, I would have to return. And it was there, from the deepest darkness, in a flash, I saw ahead of myself. Hurtling through space, faster than speed of light were the remnants of the garden wall that could become the stepping stones for a way back. I began to run, running towards as fast as I could, but the faster I went the further away I appeared. How could it be?—this prophetic moment had me chasing infinity; my heart was pounding and it was about to burst.

    With a jolt I awoke in the blinding brightness of midday sun. Eyes blinking black spots flooding with light, hand raised shielding my eyes while everything gathered itself into presence as though at beginning of time. But something remained that I could not escape; it was haunting. I rubbed my eyes awake, and my skin prickled with burn, the burning heat of dark matter entering earth's atmosphere. Open, exposed—had I lost my whereabouts? Beside me, between stones, the basket was glowing straw; and a sudden anticipation: there, inside the basket, a thin dark shadow had coiled itself. My finger chased the

shadow around the bottom of the basket,
describing the possibility of the slow worm
being there, having been there. I put the lid on,
freeing the shadow in darkness; now the basket
once empty was full of darkness. And there I
sat, the sun was shining between stones, the
basket was its own sun; I smelt warmth in straw,
but the heat was unbearable, so I picked up the
basket and went to find the shade of a tree.

    I took a leisurely path through the long
grass and along the old garden wall, stepping
on and over stones, into the orchard. The
apple trees created a canopy and there was the
plank of wood across two upturned buckets.
The atmosphere was thick. I was a child here,
I found freedom here and I sat, in the shade
of the apple trees, with my golden basket of
darkness on my lap, looking back at the garden
wall—and here was before and after coinciding
in untouched bliss and happiness.

Giving with grace
(I am because you are, we all are)

All I can say is that I felt I had to. At that time when so many appeared to be wanting to seek, establish, consolidate and defend 'their' identity what I wanted to delve into was penchants, proclivities, appetites, tastes, attractions and leanings—let's say *inclinations*—being the matter of *how* life comes about and is lived. I simply had to find a way to speak. I had to.

With the stress on *how*, I knew straightway that I needed to comprehend and appreciate inclinations not as qualities, properties or idiosyncrasies belonging to *what* life has become (and is named as) but, rather, as generative and constitutive. That's to say, it is inclinations that make a way of life. And with a way of life what is at issue is living and life itself.

For me, *inclinations* most certainly spoke of penchants, tastes, attractions and desires yet what had to be embraced was a process that goes two ways, if not more ways, at once. A body leans towards what leans its way. It's a two-way process that involves capacities—capacities to affect and to be affected. Simply put, an inclination affects what leans towards it as what it leans towards also affects it. A consequence of this two-way process is that any distinction between passive and active becomes mixed up.

And then an example presents itself to me: a fungus leaning toward roots and roots leaning towards a fungus and together, underground, affecting each other and forming a way of living. Here are inclinations—penchants, proclivities, appetites, tastes, attractions, leanings—going both ways at once and in the middle of which there is giving, nothing but giving: fugus giving water and nutrients to roots; roots giving sugars to fungus. And all of it coming to generate, constitute and thicken a form of life. Neither a fungus or roots nor anything else owns it, not even life is itself. It is nothing but *giving*. And what is to be embraced is a situation where giver and receiver truly fall together.

It would be sad, if not unjust, to make this giving fit into a model of exchange where debt—'you owe me'—is always lurking. Indeed, so many gifts have been given with the assumption that this act incurs a debt—at some point there has to be, there must be, reciprocation. The 'principle' of exchange has held sway over so much, but as David Graeber reminds me in his book *Debt: The First 5,000 Years*, 2011, exchange implies separation. He also reminds me that 'paying one's debt is not the essence of morality'. It is a cherished assumption that there is virtue in paying your debts, but let's not forget that there is an intimate relation between debt and subjection.

Exchange implies separation, I get that. However, since the moment I saw inclinations—penchants, proclivities, appetites, tastes, attractions and leanings—as generative in the making of forms that are, for life, ways of living, I have become aware that what I am seeing is the emergence of an enmeshed world, which is, even for the segregation and violence imposed upon it, indivisible. In other words, inclinations make for the embeddedness of all things in one another—I am because you are, we all are.

And what keeps coming to me is the giving where giver and receiver fall together indistinguishably and no debt is incurred. A friend said it to me: giving without debt defines grace. Giving with grace. And when I hear of the African philosophy expressed in the word 'uBunto', I feel the affirmation of not only the embeddedness and immersion of all things in one another but also giving with grace. Translations of uBunto vary yet all express the interdependence that comes with, 'I am because you are, we all are'. In her *Law and Revolution in South Africa: UBuntu, Dignity, and the Struggle for Constitutional Transformation*, 2014, Drucilla Cornell says uBuntu is an ethical demand 'to bring about a shared world' and, by definition, a shared world can't be exclusive. Going all the way it means including *everything*: I am because of the embeddedness and immersion of all things in one another.

Before

The silence is unbearable; the light is blinding; the suitcase in the middle of the room casts its shadow. Milieu. Here we are. No! Here I am. We have not arrived: I am being left, left in a safe place, a place where what is most precious can be forgotten. Abandoned. You think memory serves you well and you will return to pick up where you left off. Get on your way! time does not stand still. Tick tock, tick tock, tick tock; the past, the present, the future; from there to there to there.

— There, there, don't cry, it is not the end of the world.

The suitcase, a lump in the middle of the room. A lump in the back of my throat. The

suitcase carries all my belongings, weighed
down, tears well up; the suitcase, a monument
to me, silently communicating between two
sides, before and after... after I remembered
before silence; after I climbed trees before words
stop speaking; after I cried before forgetting;
after the cat killed the shrew before birds sing
everyday another day the same; after the water
ran fast before rubble piles high; after the night
fell before day absorbs darkness; after I was told
before time enters.

    I am just eight years old. Heaven above,
thunder underneath; the future before me
bears its own event and binds me to the spot.
Look upon this scene: the room; me, wide-eyed,
innocent. Fear and trembling! The suitcase
sits there, a block. Now! must the events of
my life be sacrificed to this moment cut
between before and after? Look around: What
is happening? Where is the angel? Where is
the ram to take my place? Unspeakable ordeal:
all is concentrated in this moment I cannot
escape. Can you not see? Do you not hear?

My life tripped in the reckoning of time, my words stumble. What can I do? Before now I was innocent, before now there was no after, before now this word before did not exist. Speak up! What can I say? Before now is silent: my innocence, already bound to before, is lost to after; time has entered and must I account for it? Speak up! Torn apart, now is silent with only the noise of my own breathing.

Before now and after; the silence was unbearable, the light was blinding. My mother took the largest suitcase. My mother chose what to pack. My mother folded each item carefully. My mother did not know I loved my orange t-shirt. My mother closed the suitcase trapping smell and dark space around my belongings. My mother wrote my name on the label. My mother carried the suitcase downstairs. My mother put the suitcase in the car. My mother told me to get in the car. (What was she thinking?) My mother shouted get in the car.

My mother sat in the car waiting for me, door open, radio on. My mother did not say a word. Then she began to drive. Then her words poured out over the radio, inside the radio, around switching channels, poor reception: was I listening? was I hearing? did I understand? could I understand? my mother's voice, a blurred landscape all noise. Then we were there. My mother parked the car. My mother carried the suitcase up the long, deep steps (that was 24 two-step steps) to the boarding house. My mother waited. My mother was shown into a room. My mother put the suitcase in the middle of the room. And the silence was unbearable, and the light was blinding. And my mother left me there.

— There, there, don't cry, it is not the end of the world.

There, there was not the voice of my mother; there, there was not a world I recognized; there, there was foreign; there, there language gave back no words; there, there separated my being in the world. There, the suitcase, its shadow pushing darkness into the room, light caught in tears. There, the boarding house. Who carried the suitcase to the dormitory; who opened the suitcase; who placed my belongings in ordered piles onto the bed; who called the inventory; who took my hand? There, there was a small voice belonging to a memory only a memory and whose memory was it?

I was eight years old, taken from there, I did not know there could be separated from there; I did not know the ground could lose its ground; I did not know I did not yet recognize myself; I did not know there was a passage of time. Adrift. I cried and I cried and I cried. Before enwreathed with darkness, then shadows rose and fell, I did not know there was no time limit to this process. Left in the lurch, never again could I not know.

— There, there, don't cry, we are all in the same boat.

There and then; the silence is unbearable,

the light is blinding. The suitcase is open, my belongings laid out. There around each item, inside each fold, each wrap, each touch is my mother's work; dark space and smell turning memory. Then I cry, cry for mother, cry for home, cry for before; emotion floats in every direction. Settle down, settle down. There I am, derelict and there is my shadow. There is the suitcase, emptied and there is the label with my name on it.

There and then in the same boat, sharing the same fate, 64 children in a boarding house there, there unlocatable and eternal. There and then I cry. There and then I cry I want to go home. There and then we are in the same boat. We. Who is this we that I now belong to? Speak up! There and then I cry. There and then I want to go home. There and then we are in the same boat. We. Will anyone speak up for me? There and then we cry we want to go home now. Now! an indeterminate time; we, a dissociated I on the open sea, black swell without shore; now wash away the tears, homesickness makes us nauseous. We are all in the same boat. We. We smell of coal tar soap.

— Settle down, settle down, don't rock the boat.
    Now here we all are, shipshape and squeaky clean, confined to a safe place; the boarding house, all exits locked and no place to flee to. I am not staying. Altruism moves between us enclosing a mutinous self (find me if you can) as now is placated with the promise of a better tomorrow. I refuse to wait. Coal tar catches the back of the throat: I was eight years old: here is the suitcase, here is the label with my name on it: and Now! every moment is my escape.

We need to make another future (Radical love)

Capitalism in all its variations and incarnations continues to create ever more 'misery, oppression, slavery, degradation and exploitation'. Marx predicted the likelihood and he wrote these very words for the first publication of *Capital Volume 1* in 1867. And all for profit, the maximization of it and, furthermore, bolstered by the conviction that the 'market' is the highest form of human freedom.

... closed markets, free markets, global markets, financial markets, capital markets, regulated, deregulated, unregulated; elimination of controls, state intervention, minimum of state intervention; state and markets hand in hand, commercialization, marketization (Higher Education for example); domination of financial institutions, credit money, profiting from debt and more debt and more profit, market sovereignty; planet earth treated as private resource, shareholders over those who toil, an elite class of central bankers, financiers and corporate executives ... globalization, neoliberalism, financialization and the coming of corporate sovereignty, mega private companies owned by a few and a law unto themselves.

I can see no beauty in this.

And love?

I am prepared to speak about love. But what preparation do I need? The only answer I have is love—it is love that lets me see where there is no love. I am prepared to speak about communism. Communism and love? With communism ceasing to be pinned down as an ideological (re)organization of economic 'life', I can say that there is no distance between communism and love. I can say, they fall into one another.

In the face of aggression, racism, division and segregation, Martin Luther King was prepared to speak about love. He had decided to love, to 'stick with love'. In 1967 he said it emphatically, 'I'm not taking about emotional bosh'. A year later, Martin Luther King was assassinated, a hundred and one years since Marx spoke of capitalism's capacity to create ever more 'misery, oppression, slavery, degradation and exploitation'. The earth is wretched without love.

The anonymous French collective The Invisible Committee were prepared to speak about communism—and love. In *Now*, 2017, they speak of 'us' but they also frequently say 'I'. They say that communism is a question of how to live. They say that what is utopian in communism dates back at least to the prophets of Jewish antiquity. *The Book of Psalms* becomes quoted, and here are words for the future:

'And equal land for all, divided not/By walls or fences, … and the course/Of life be common and wealth unapportioned./For there no longer will be poor nor rich,/Tyrant nor slave, nor any great nor small,/Nor kings nor leaders; all alike in common/'

But there's a problem with how the question of communism has been framed. The Invisible Committee say that it has been framed as a *strictly human* question. The question of communism has never stopped troubling the world, for it stems from 'a basic, immemorial, lived experience: that of *community*'. Community is not an entity to which I belong; it is an experience of *continuity* between beings and with world. They say that in love, in friendship, we experience that continuity. With love there is not one and the other and between them a love relation. There is only direct contact and mingling indistinctly—that's the experience of continuity be it with a little piece of the world of which I am part and which is also a part of me. And there is ample beauty in this.

Come 2019, just as a pandemic is to rip through the world, Grace Blakley is wasting no time in telling us just how finance capitalism dumped on so many; stole so much, even the future. At the very end of her *Stolen: How to Save the World from Financialisation*, she says we have let our futures be determined by the wealthy and the hope that they would use their influence for the good of the whole. Self-interested, exploitative and reckless is how she describes an elite, politicians included, who would rather see the planet burn than sacrifice 'an iota of their wealth'. In 2019 another future was needed, and it still is.

The Earth is indeed wretched without love. Yes, I am prepared to speak about love and love demands that I see what gives no love—and how! It is personal yet more than personal. It is *critical*. It is to see the misery, sickness, denigration and unhappiness that capitalism continues to inflict and, with that, the breakdown of people, planet, climate and yet to *not* go for that future but instead to find, make and cherish that other future, which might well come from the past. And then I flip back to the future that, in 1994, is waiting to be born with the words and profound conviction of bell hooks in *Love as the Practice of Freedom*. It's love shaping the direction of and being the foundation of a political vision: 'Without love, our efforts to liberate ourselves and our world community from oppression and exploitations are doomed.'

Love is the best chance we have 'to cease allegiance to systems of domination—imperialism, sexism, racism, classism'. Loves gives us the best position from which

We need to make another future (Radical love)   *79*

to do something about the problems facing the entire planet. The future that I've gone back to lets me talk back and say:

We need radical love.

Sentimental?

—*Really?*

Admit it: market-based solutions haven't worked and they are not going to work.

Ever more dense

From a cliff edge: waves rise over the horizon, it is rough at sea. Coming in and out, high and low, breaking waves erode the cliff bottom up; the cliff overhangs. Jagged lines. Sky meets sea, sea meets shore, shore meets cliff, cliff meets sky. The wind picks up, clouds swell black, heavy swells break, on and on and on. Waves pound the cliff. Carried by the tide, the sea runs in rising and falling, the sea falls off leaving a slither of shore, the cliff ground down, worn down. And exposed are the petrified remains, the traces of ancient life, plant and animal waiting for freedom. From a cliff edge: clouds swell black, rain takes away my tears; all that energy frothing water, I jump into the unforgettable, the gap between past and future.

Paradise (The walls of incarceration falling)

In the ancient Iranian language of Avestan, known through Zoroastrian scripture, paradise—*pairidaeza*—is a spacious walled garden—*pairi* meaning 'around' and *daeza* meaning 'wall'. Greek language borrows the word and *paradeisos* appears in the Septuagint, the earliest Greek translation of the Hebrew Bible known as the Old Testament. Coming to describe the divine Garden of Eden in Genesis, paradise furnished Christianity with a powerful imaginary: God planted paradise in Eden where, before anything else, Adam and Eve lived naked and roamed freely. But in this earthly paradise, this original dwelling place of humanity, temptation is given into and the forbidden fruit of the tree of knowledge is eaten. Disobedience and guilt lead to the Fall, bringing sin and corruption to humanity and nature and, with that, expulsion from paradise and shame of nakedness (women take the blame for this). In the early centuries of Christianity, the theologian Augustine has this Fall constitute the doctrine of original sin. It is here that the

Church necessitates itself—with original sin (a truly sad idea if there ever was one), the salvation and redemption dispensed by the Church becomes essential and, moreover, constitutes its power.

The walls that surround the Persian garden and make *pairidaeza* were erected to keep out the weeds and the wild—you could even say, the 'uncivilized'. Quite the opposite are the walls, fences and barriers built for incarceration; these erections and installations are to keep in. It's prison. Bottom line, prisons are walls, fences, barriers and *a power to punish*. In 1975 Michael Foucault says as much. In his *Discipline and Punishment: The Birth of the Prison* he also says that the emergence of the prison marks the institutionalization of the power to punish.

With that institutionalization, prison and the power to punish are in the hands of the State, even if in neoliberal times the carceral apparatus—the building, design, finance and the day-to-day running of—is marketized, that's to say privatized. Unlike the public spectacle of hanging or whipping or branding or locking into stocks, the prison is the place where the power to punish doesn't dare to manifest itself. Even if the fence is thin and latticed and the barriers electronic and for all the 'rehabilitation', the coercion that happens when you're inside doing time is kept out of view.

In a small volume called *The Kingdom and the Garden*,

Paradise (The walls of incarceration falling)

2020, the Italian philosopher Giorgio Agamben tells of paradise as set forth by the medieval Irish theologian and poet Scotus Eriugena: earthly paradise is not lost forever in the past; rather, humanity has never yet been in paradise. It goes something like this: there is a radical unity between humanity and all living things, all of life, and this unity is the true nature of humanity, which is paradise itself; but humanity has not yet known its true nature, has not yet known paradise. The true nature of humanity (paradise) is the unity of life beyond any division and, what is more, utterly without walls. It is a life common to all, 'a potential that nourishes and increases all that is born from the earth'. For me, this paradise is to be born together no matter distances, temporal or spatial; it is all forms of life as the *potential* of life.

The thought of being incarcerated in paradise seems paradoxical if not stupid, but if *this* paradise is where walls and not humanity fall perhaps it is not so stupid. With the paradise that is radically without walls, where the unity of life beyond division is the true nature of humanity, you will see incarceration stripped back and that's to see it starkly—I want to say, nakedly. With nothing masking or obfuscating, the violence of the state and the normalization of it is there to see. That's the coercive forces that sustain the power to punish. That's the police, the criminal courts, the border controls. It is also prejudice, you name it—racial, gender—how you dress—the migrant, the refugee—the interests and maintenance of a ruling class—criminalization of poverty, ill health, homelessness and being unable; and then, the entanglement of capitalism's insatiable want of profit—build more prisons no matter what.

From the situation of paradise, the profound unity of all born together on this Earth, you see incarceration starkly; it is fully exposed and with that you see things maybe you didn't expect to see. You see a past that hasn't been obliterated. You see ships, hundreds of ships. Yes, ships built to incarcerate. Yes, here is years and years of the transatlantic slave trade. It is all exposed. The transatlantic slave trade giving rise to the transatlantic capitalist system, and that's men, women and children reduced to, stolen and sold to become, enslaved commodities. And then there is the punishment. The unending night and day punishment. Not only hell in the form of those incarcerating ships and those confining colonial plantations and their authoritarian masters but also, on top of that, sustained brutality and cruelty: beatings, branding, torture and rape.

What was all this punishment for?

For the reason that the colour of this body made it punishable. For reasons of the lie of 'racial' inferiority. For the reason that this body, man, women or child, could be exploited and done with in any way whatsoever wanted. Exploitation—yes. Denigration—yes. And add to this, racialization bringing segregation and hatred, none of which goes away as slavery is abolished. With walls, fences and barriers falling, paradise lets me see incarceration fully exposed and, what's more, lets me see the manufactured character of race unmasked—nothing is concealing it.

Paradise is the unity of life, all forms of life as the *potential* of life. And paradise (potential) *materializes* everywhere, including the air, the wind and waters. It is time for humanity to fully see paradise, its true nature. Paradise hides nothing and is nowhere hidden. Paradise is there in her face (that face that is punched because of wanton violence). Paradise is there with that body (that body that's been raped and left crumpled on the floor). Paradise hides nothing and is nowhere hidden and this is what makes paradise an exposing force, a questioning force—of that punch, of that rape, of that racialization, of that determination to separate and segregate, to harden borders and identities. Paradise is that tree over a thousand years, still growing and having seen so much.

—'Hey, the walls of prisons don't need building.'

Over time

The children knelt, each on a sheet of newspaper, each tending to a small patch of flowerbed. The flowerbed, there was only one, it edged a grassy mound and there was only one grassy mound, it concealed the old air-raid shelter. There was hush, no talking.

    The teacher stood sentry next to the wheelbarrow, the large rusty wheelbarrow that carried everything from the potting shed to the flowerbed and back again. Loaded up with tools, paper, seedlings, mulch and watering can, pushed by two children, one on each handle, its wheel wobbled, squeaked, jammed; the children would push, it teetered; the teacher would proclaim an object lesson in joint effort and balance.

For an hour, every other Saturday afternoon,
unless it was too wet to kneel or so cold the
earth froze, the children weeded, trowelled and
planted the flowerbed. The teacher would leave
her post purposefully to inspect; her shadow
loomed over each child, she breathed ideal—a
well-kept flowerbed blooms with cultivation;
there is no place for weeds; effort now, reward
later; pitiful blooms are penalty for ignorance;
good habits protect your future. Turning over
the soil, digesting the lesson, uncertainty and
doubt raked and scraped against the children's
diligence.

Weeds: wild, inferior and unwanted.
Weeds have no place in God's garden, so it
was said. Weeds must be pulled from the roots,
nothing must be left behind, so it was said.
Weeds, like bad habits, return again and again,
history shows this to be true, so it was said.
Some understand this better than others,
so it was said.

The smell of the earth wafting down among
the roots unleashed a synthesis between past

and future: fresh rot rising. Extracted and strewn over the newspaper, tangles of roots clinging to bits of soil, green shoots, flowers to be: is that a weed, was that a weed? Planting itself amongst newspaper print, letters and text, a whisper of a flower before it will have been.

How were they to know? Fearing a temptation of a backward glance, the future bore into them. Orange, blue petals, yellow petals, pink; a large bee flying around aimless; stems and leaves nibbled; sunlight in and out, buds open to flowers seeing without words; faces; crumbly soil, a stretched worm bulging blood; picking dirt from under fingernails, touching sensations; green stingers, feeling without words. The children knew many things, they could count and write their name, but sensations, filled with sensations, the children felt but they had no words for how they felt; the children saw without direction but they had no words for what was what. A ring of emotion, a palpable sense of loss surrounded the air-raid shelter.

Without a word. Lessons were being learned, lessons found in everything. The air-raid shelter bordered by a flowerbed, divided; each child tending their own, each looking to each other, left and right, friend or not, sharing or not, caring or not, kind or not; divided, a blooming flower or a weed left out to die. Without a word. A sharp intake of breath singled out; teacher's favourite or not; criticism, a dark cloud passing; praise, a sun shining warm; in or out examples were made.

The children knelt, the precariousness of their knowledge felt natural, as natural as a dead woodlouse on its back, but they didn't know what natural was. It was the teacher who assumed knowingness; she had seen it all before, she had the past behind her. And she pointed her finger. She was the teacher pointing out that and that, rights and wrongs; and in her other hand she held a stone. This was how it was to be: as predictable as the seasons, as sure as there is night and day. And she did, where she found failure, place a stone; stones that made an example of, stones that put an end to the unexpected, stones that were not to be moved. Every year the flowerbed dotted with stones; stony faced, hers was a disabling perfectionism and the children learnt this.

That was then and sheltered underneath the stones were woodlice and worms digesting what could have been. And the flowerbed looked pretty and the grassy mound proud; and the children learnt a past never to be forgotten. Overhead bombs fell, air-raid sirens wailed, the people ran to the shelter buried underground, six to a bench, in the dark; and they would emerge to clear skies, before and after returning to before, and the bombs fell and the sirens wailed, they ran to the shelter and emerging from the dark the bombs fell and the sirens wailed. High above, overhead, in the sky, across a world, through night and day: monumental times, monumental men: us and them, allies and enemies, heroes and villains. War. Before the war. After the war. Never forget, never forget this great past: the bombs fell and the sirens

wailed this vicious cycle. And of course the
teacher lived through the war, before and after;
revelling in a history heaped up with facts and
dates, she buried the children alive in the past:
if it had not been for such and such, if it had not
been for so and so, if it had not been.

And the sirens wail. And the children kneel,
each on a sheet of newspaper, each tending
to a small patch of flowerbed. The flowerbed,
there is only one, it edges a grassy mound and
there is only one grassy mound, it conceals the
old air-raid shelter. There is hush, no talking.
Beside themselves: silently flowers bloom and
stones constellate spaces between; and what
remains is a darkness sheltering that without
description, without before or after.

A rigorous innocence (The cry of the world)

I have no entitlement. None. But I can think. And perhaps because I have no entitlement is why I can think.

—Where do I get this idea from?

Entitlement is you assuming that because you are you, you get to have what you believe is yours; it is you assuming that because you are you, you are at liberty to do what you want with whatever or whomever. As I dig around to find out 'how come?', I soon realize that entitlement is built on thin air and hides this from itself—it becomes something like a blind spot. Because of this, entitlement doesn't think itself and doesn't think beyond itself. Entitlement stops short of thinking—if this were not the case then how come domestic violence continues to happen?

Violence can indeed be taken as a form of entitlement. I can't think it otherwise: entitlement, that unquestioned sense of entitlement, was party to the unleashing of colonialism upon the world and the prejudice of racism that came with it, which prevails still to this day. And then there is the dictator puffed up big with entitlement. Yet it could be anyone, just anyone: entitlement not thinking itself, not thinking beyond itself.

I can't gag myself: entitlement doesn't think about the losses and destruction inflicted by humanity on the Earth—the loss of plants, insects, fauna, habitats. Humanity is a big word, I know that; nonetheless, whatever the entitlement that has arisen under and because of that designation needs to disappear. It is for 'humanity' to be born again and this time *to be born with others*—an otherwise living soul sharing the same soul as, and indistinguishable from, all others born of life and the Earth, climates and rivers and winds included. The very idea and *reality* of being born together solicits thinking that thinks yourself and beyond yourself; it is a thinking that neither condemns nor absolves; it is, as the philosopher Gilles Deleuze once said, a 'rigorous innocence'.

To be *truly* thinking surely is to be thinking without prejudice or pre-established criteria—this is a rigorous innocence and for that reason immediately political. With a rigorous innocence there is no thinking premised on an identity—'either you are male or female'. Being born together is to think the inclinations of everything; it is to think the leanings of our sexualities at the same time as the leanings of the sexualities of others. No pre-established criteria and no premises. This thinking doesn't condemn or absolve and it comes with making room—yet never taking over. Yes, being born together solicits thinking that is a rigorous innocence and, whatever the sexual leaning, entitlement is out of the picture.

I had awoken suddenly in the middle of night after having dreamt I saw the assassination of Rosa Luxemburg, activist, theorist, journalist, socialist revolutionary, public speaker, Polish, German, Jewish. I saw her carried out of a hotel, with blood streaming from her mouth and nose, by what looked like paramilitaries and shoved into the back of a car. The car drove off and there on the running board was a figure and he fired a shot. A bullet straight to her head. 47 years old. Her body was then dumped in a nearby canal. It's Berlin, 15 January 1916. I was there but I was not there. I felt like a ghost from the future.

Rosa Luxemburg cared passionately about the future: an emancipated society, a world without exploitation, without alienation and without borders. This woman was shot in the head for the reason she never stopped short of thinking. Whatever she wrote, from personal letters in prison to pamphlets and books, Rosa Luxemburg did not stop short of thinking. She did not stop short of thinking in the face of authoritarianism and the oppression of capitalism. She did not stop short of thinking in the face of nationalism, militarism, chauvinism, dogmatism, racism and xenophobia. And in a pamphlet called *The Russian*

Revolution, 1918, there are words to be found that have become much quoted: 'Freedom is always and exclusively freedom for the one who thinks differently.'

As I stay with these words, what begins to emerge is the rigorous innocence with which entitlement is out of the picture. Freedom for the one who thinks differently is no one taking over, no one cajoling and saying that there is only one way to think. It is thinking *here* and *there* at the very same time and letting the diversity of the world flourish, without which it shrinks, shrivels and ultimately dies. With that said I begin to hear a cry, at first faint but becoming louder and louder. Is this cry coming from the past or from the future? Both. It is the cry that the poet and thinker Édouard Glissant wants us to hear and listen to throughout *The Treatise of the Whole-World (Traité du tout-monde)*, 1997. It is the cry of the world.

'To listen to the cry of the world—not theories, ideologies or power ... but the huge entanglement where one neither sacrifices oneself in lamentations nor gets carried away with hopes.' The cry of the world is the diversity of the all-world or the whole-world, *tout-monde* as he would say, and its beauty 'explodes in the entanglement'. And listening to the cry of the world we know we are no longer able to sing, speak or work without others.

And then I'm stopped in my tracks by the realization that in those much-quoted words of Rosa Luxemburg, written in prison and perhaps less than year before her murder, it is the whole world speaking to her through, as Édouard Glissant would say, 'so many gagged voices'.

Memory

She had been walking for a long time before
she came upon the tree. The tree, a fine tree
particular to itself, made her instantly happy.
She followed its base, looked up through the
branches, placed her hands on the trunk;
the emotion she felt was something akin to
meeting a friend for the first time; she would be
returning here, again and again.

    Fortune had it that there was a bench
beside the tree where she could sit quietly in
its presence though her visits would not go
unnoticed. The tree, situated on the fringes of
a significant location, was looked upon in all
directions. Windows everywhere and passers-
by; but who might be watching would not be
her concern.

Well now, she was seen. Who could she possibly be, this stranger who had come from somewhere else? There was no end of conjecture but observing from a distance how far could an imagination go with an unknown woman sitting on a bench next to a tree? There was a limit and it was not long before she was no longer a talking point. They, whoever they were, stopped seeing her, forgot to notice her. She, the bench, the tree, became inseparable, absorbed into time passing. And she, whoever she was to them, fell silent; she no longer stood out and no one could remember she had not gone away; she had, as it were, become immortal.

Now again, she is sitting on the bench next to the tree. The tree mute, bare branches extending out, awaits the possibility of its name. Say spring, say April, and a wind blows; blossom is falling, covering the ground, covering the bench. Without word, what can be seen, what can be heard, is a pattern of agains —billowy blooms, transient beauty, drifts. And what has language got to say? Cherry blossom falls silent.

Memory

    Now again, she is sitting on the bench next to the tree. For her, who has come from somewhere else, the tree had come from out of the blue. And she felt the memory of her first encounter with the tree physically—such happiness, such happiness—yet could she keep it, what language would serve to remind? Oh, the lament! Returning and returning to contain a memory after it's no longer reachable yet remains unforgettable—cherry blossom.

    Now again, she is sitting on the bench next to the tree. Wasting time? Time is passing, seasons have come and gone, the tree blossoms and blossom falls. Again and again, she sits on the bench; she, the bench, the tree, are inseparable—such happiness, such happiness—this is the stuff of memory! Musing what is or has been, thought from somewhere else, memory follows, yet what needs remembering, and perpetually forgotten, remains silently here awaiting its possibility.

Don't forget language (Remembering the indivisible)

More and more am I hearing it said that the Earth, and that's also to say Nature, which we are all born into, is indivisible, and that the wilful, if not venal, ignorance of this is doing harm. Knowing of the indivisibility of Earth/Nature, its fragility and tenacity, is not by any means new—peoples past have cared for it and lived it. Today I am remembering Spinoza, seventeenth-century philosopher. I am remembering his 'single indivisible substance'. And this substance, call it *Natura*, has infinite modes—all 'creatures' are this including trees, flowers, mountain streams and seas. *Natura*: Spinoza's God is internal to this.

Here's the thing about this single indivisible substance: it doesn't exist elsewhere than in the multiplicity of its modes. This substance doesn't refer to stuff and doesn't divide into parts, as you would expect; rather it folds into modes, modifying itself—you could say, *Natura* 'naturing itself'. What I hold dear is that here I am folded into an unbounded whole and, with it, there is no 'external' place for a transcendent creator or power. It is political. Spinoza's indivisible substance is not and never will be a 'world of things'.

But what about language? What about language and the indivisibility of Earth/Nature? Do we give any thought to or even care about language keeping us close and even closer to Earth/Nature? I'm in the presence of all languages on Earth and I'm not forgetting this plurality as I go to address these questions with the case of *something being said about something*. As for example, 'Moss, that most ancient of plants, is a vibrant green.'

Something is being said about something. What I detect here, between the something and the something said of it, is enough space for there to be a distance. With that distance there is little stopping us imagining a world of things and language as separate from it yet saying something about it. And any idea of language getting close to this world becomes a matter of the perfection of what is said about it. But wait. Perhaps the Earth/Nature had already been seen as a world of things and obliged language to say something about it.

Things happen when Earth/Nature is seen as and *treated* as a world of things. Characteristic of a world of things is the separation of one thing from another and this is all that is needed for isolation to happen, to be made to happen. And with isolation, loneliness is never far away.

Loneliness is amongst the most desperate of experiences and this is not for only human life. Loneliness can be made to happen; it can be orchestrated. I can't forget the words of Hannah Arendt at the end of *The Origins of Totalitarianism*, 1951; she says that loneliness is what totalitarianism bases itself on; it is an experience of not belonging, of being utterly lost. Totalitarianism: none outside the state, none against the state. No opposition, no talking back, no community. Coercion, repression, subordination. And all of it total. Yes, I can't forget the 'devasting sand storm' of totalitarian rule. I can't forget. I can't.

And I can't forget language. I can't forget indivisibility. I can't. Then I remember when language isn't to be found saying something about something, and it arises with what linguistics call the nominal sentence. Nominal· names. The nominal sentence is utterly distinct from the verbal sentence and happens when the 'something' and the 'something said about it' come to fall together and no space is left to be filled by the copula 'is' or the insertion of a verb.

Snow white.

Morning sun sparkle the sea.

With nominal sentences, you find no separation, no distance between; simply put, there is no world of things, rather, a world of *indivisible events*: snow-being-white, sun-morning-sparkle-sea.

With the nominal sentence what is explicit is announcement. Names are announcing 'snow, white, sun, morning, sparkle, sea' and what's not at all hidden with this announcement is that language is also announcing itself. In being called 'sun' or 'snow', what is named by these names is announced in language and, with that, appears in language. And that is really to say: appears as language. It means that what is named by the name 'sun' or 'snow' has become sayable, has sayability. No one talks about this much today, but the ancient Stoics were well aware of the 'sayable', they called it *lekton*.

With the sayable, what is key is appearing as language and that is nothing like denoting or signifying; rather, language and what is named by a name *fold* together. It is an event for sure and hard to grasp (like all events), yet what is mirific with it is that no division ever takes place. No world of things. No separation. No isolation. For an instant, a slither of time that is immeasurable, we can experience an indivisibility between language and Earth/Nature. And what there is to care for with this experience is an unbounded indivisible whole that never shall become a totality.

Postscript
The sayable is in fact present in every sentence that says something about something, every verbal sentence,

every electronic message fired off saying stuff about ourselves or relaying an opinion; yet, time and time again, we overlook and forget this.

Gesture

In the dark, in silence, I was thinking along these lines, only to find I was in a crack. These lines: in the dark, in silence.

The wall surrounding the house, the path leading to the house, the house; cracks in the house, in the path, in the wall—don't they just appear as though they have always been there. Cracks, manifestation of movement that is for the time being and at the same time without end, particular to here and at the same time from elsewhere. Dark lines open enough for seed to take root; earth worms its way in, tufts of grass, budding weeds spill out; there is all kinds of living here. Earthly and unearthly.
 Who knocks on the front door, not just

once but many times and using a fist too? Sound, urgent and impatient, pushes its way through the house dissipating in each room. Then comes the clack of the letterbox. Who looks through the opening into the dark hallway and when there is only light enough for vague shadows to dance in and out of the darkness, who shouts—Is there anyone in? And after all this gesturing against a closed door what remains on both sides of the door is a demand to appear.

    Patience is needed here, patience for the time it takes to answer a door, an eternal time, and even an instant can take that long: now is stretching, patience is time lapsed.

It was a beautiful day, my future lay ahead of me—such confidence!—life was going to plan, I was so sure. Yet it was on this day when the sun was shining down on me that I felt a strange chill, a shadow passing over me, dark and silent. Perplexed, I decided to take a walk. Before long I reached the old pier; there projecting out to sea, a straight line towards the horizon; there the sunniest of days, fluffy clouds, sea air and for a moment my heart filled with joy.

The old pier built for pleasure, a wonder of attraction, once wood now iron, carrying to and from the shore changing times, the good old days entertaining more of this and more of that present-day. Its heritage, a mile stretch to escape it all. Gulls circle above, excited shrieks rent the air; a family day out sauntering, taking a breather, benches occupied; someone is always fishing.

On the pier, above and out to sea, looking forward, looking back, either way, all around everything was in motion—sea breeze, sun glitter on wavelets, clouds floating high—it was a beautiful day and I was somewhere in the middle of it. Free of myself, my senses deepened to the moment and nothing else. And I wished for this to be for all time, but there in sight was the end of the pier and the horizon as far and as close as could be, and there a shadow cast: my wish was without a way.

How long did I stand staring out to sea before a boat appeared, as if from nowhere, sitting on the horizon and then another sailing inland and then how many more. Out there, the end of my world, that line, a crack between sea and sky marking a limit from nowhere to somewhere; before long I would turn and be walking back to shore.

I took my time lingering around the few brightly coloured huts selling ice cream and souvenirs, yet what caught my attention was a shepherd's hut, the reading rooms of a clairvoyant decorated with all kinds of promise. The door was open and a curtain drawn back just enough to see inside. There, in subdued light, was a small round table covered with a black cloth, a large opaque crystal ball, a stool to sit on and the clairvoyant sitting opposite. Something from before impelled me to enter.

The atmosphere was close. I placed both hands on the table palms up. The clairvoyant took my hands in hers. Then with her index finger she followed the lines on my right palm.

Gesture

She began her reading. In those lines she saw what was coming and it was there, fleeing from the present, that I would encounter myself understanding life without consequence. In my hands time lapsed; lines dark and silent held the movement of life, every possible instant, never-ending.

It was as if I had been shown a secret that was my life!—a life made of gestures and words, calling silently, opaque and unjudgeable. As I walked out into the open, life and language fell together and I reflected how free I felt.

A day out on the pier leaves nothing behind.

And the door—has it been answered? A question, a ceaseless interruption, appears to be left standing either side of the door. The door, an invocation to appear. But a black line around the door outlines an empty space, neither open nor closed, and impassable. But there a space of freedom becomes possible, opening for itself: I, alone with my words; in the dark, in silence.

A life worth living (Free will collapsed)

Was her life worth living? Whichever way she went there were hoops to go through. Each hoop she had to go through called her into question; in fact, these hoops had built into them 'to be at fault' and leading inexorably to assessment and judgement. For any help she needed and sought she would be judged, and just a hair's breadth away there was always blame and accusation. She felt her life had become one long continuous trial. Even the devil thought it hell and objected—it is time for the elimination of accusation and a judgemental God.

Oh to be done with judgement!

But it seems we are nowhere near being done with judgement. With all those ticks, hearts, likes, dislikes, thumbs up and thumbs down, we are doing it daily to ourselves. With an insatiable appetite for visibility and a fear of being ignored, we can't stop looking, can't stop appearing—hey, look at me, see what I've done. Social media. Internet life. Everyone is watching everyone else. Everyone is judging. And it brings elation, misery, the glory of adulation, the hell of dejection. Riposte: at least we are doing it of our own free will.

Free will? There is nothing innocent let alone natural about free will; it is an invention, elaborated over time, of Christian theology. It comes down to this: endowed with a will, a *free will*, you and I bear all the responsibility for what we do—our actions are imputable. As subjects having free will, we are from the very start constituted as culpable.

I get it why some refer to free will as an 'apparatus' and a neat one at that. The function of this 'theological apparatus' is clear: it introduces into the world a mechanism that secures your responsibility to your action and ties you down and holds you there (no plunging into chaos). You are converted into a moral subject and held accountable and culpable for your actions. Free will is an ingenious apparatus: fault lies within you, you are wholly judgeable and, moreover, always on trial. Where is the joy in all of this?

I say it without belligerence: I don't have a will that directs what I can do—when she says that *she can*, she is announcing that she is a being of potential. She can do because she is able. She can do because of capacities. There is a world of difference between *I can* and *I will*, but in Western culture, *will* has taken over from *can* and, what's more, this 'take over' marks a passage. A passage in Western culture, from an ancient world to a modern world. In this ancient world she is a being whose thoughts and actions are all about potential and she is responsible because she is able. In this ancient world, if I do bad stuff it is because I am ignorant, but in a modern world it is because of an act of will, which from the very start makes me blameworthy.

With the passage from *I can* to *I will*, there is nothing stopping me from crossing back into that ancient world of potential to bring it forward, not to bring it up to date but, rather, to show that we—the Earth/Nature—have never stopped *being* potential. The free will that would make each of us the owner of our actions, making us culpable and privatizing our existences, doesn't exist. It never has—but what a fiction. And how we have fallen for it.

She has been spun around and, in the process, come to understand—it has been an experience—that what I can do and how I can be is inextricably bound up with a capacity to be affected. We have a capacity to affect one another and what is key is that it involves our powers of action and being. Potential is to be able; it is also power. It is not 'will' that makes us; rather, it is a *power* to be affected. And an ethics begins here without any moral subject being introduced: the greater the power to be affected (the greater my receptivity), the greater the power of action and being, and this goes for all involved—both selfishness and altruism are out of the window. And as those powers and capacities increase we can go from sadness and suffering to joy; it is a passage and 'free will' doesn't come into it. But what does is the living of a life that is not continuously on trial. That's a life worth living.

What our times really call for is an opening onto other ways of experiencing time and space.
—Achilles Mbembe

For all other editions, please visit the Copy Press website --
www.copypress.co.uk